The Fairy Tale Bedtime Collection

® Landoll, Inc.
© 1996 Landoll, Inc.
Ashland, Ohio 44805

Table of Contents

The Emperor's New Clothes

retold by Diane Stortz

Fairy Tale Classics

Many years ago, in a faraway land, there ruled an emperor who loved clothes. He had a different outfit for every hour of every day. He never left his dressing room except to ride through the kingdom in his carriage to show off his clothes. Tailors and seamstresses came from all over the world to show the king the latest colors and designs.

ne day, two tricksters came to the palace. They said they were weavers.

"Dear emperor," they said. "We have come to tell you about the most fantastic fabric in the world. It is fine, light, and beautiful and people who are stupid or unfit for their jobs can not see it! Just think! If you had clothes made of this special fabric, you would discover which men in the kingdom are unfit for their offices. You would be able to tell the fools from the wise."

"Oh, quite right," said the emperor, and he paid the two tricksters a lot of money in advance to make him a suit of this wonderful cloth.

The tricksters asked for spools of silk and pure gold thread. They set up two looms in an empty shop in the middle of the kingdom. The spools of silk and pure gold thread went into the tricksters' bags, not on the looms. Then the two sat at their empty looms and pretended to weave, long into the night.

he next day, the emperor wanted to see the cloth. But he was a tiny bit afraid that he might be unfit for his position, and if that were true, he did not want anyone to know it. So instead of going to the weavers' shop himself, the emperor sent his most trusted advisor.

he advisor could see nothing, of course, since there wasn't anything to see. "Dear me," the advisor said to himself. "Does this mean that I am a fool? I can not tell the emperor that I can not see the cloth!" So he went back to the emperor and reported that the cloth was indeed beautiful.

he emperor soon sent another of his faithful officials to see the weavers' cloth. Of course that man could see nothing either, but he did not want to admit this to anyone. "How can it be that I am a fool?" he wondered. So he assured the weavers that the cloth was lovely and he told the emperor that his new clothes were going to be splendid.

The emperor decided that he wanted to see this magnificent fabric while it was still on the loom. So he called the royal court to go with him to the weaver's shop. The tricksters were working away as hard as ever at their empty looms when the emperor and the royal court arrived.

The weavers showed the emperor the invisible fabric. The emperor looked at the weavers, and then at the members of the royal court. "The fabric is marvelous your Majesty," they all began to say. "Quite amazing! Splendiferous! What design! What colors!"

The emperor was dismayed. "Can they all see what I can not see?" he thought. "Am I unfit for my position? Am I a fool? I must not let anyone know!" Then he pretended to feel the fine fabric and admire its colors and patterns along with everyone else.

The tricksters promised to complete the emperor's new suit by morning. "Why not have a procession to let all of your subjects see your wonderful new clothes?" they suggested. The emperor agreed.

That night, the tricksters burned sixteen candles while they sat up and pretended to cut and sew the invisible cloth. In the morning, they took the invisible clothes to the palace. "Here is the coat," they said, pretending to hold something up to be seen. "These are the trousers, and this is the shirt."

The emperor undressed and put on the new clothes, atleast he pretended to put them on. "How well the emperor looks in his new clothes," said all the members of the royal court, for no one was willing to admit that he could not see a thing.

The procession began. The emperor's chamberlains walked behind him, pretending to hold up the long train of his coat. All the people in the kingdom stood along the roads to see the emperor and his new clothes.

"How beautiful the emperor's clothes are!" said the people as the procession passed by. "What a wonderful fit! How elegant!" None of them wanted to be thought a fool either.

The two tricksters laughed all the way out of town with their bags full of silk and golden thread and the money the king had paid for his new clothes.

The procession continued. Then one little child pulled on his father's coat and said, "But Papa, the emperor has nothing on." "Nothing on?" repeated the boy's father. "The emperor has nothing on!" all the people cried at last.

he emperor knew it was true, but the parade continued through the town and back to the palace. What else could he do? He certainly did not want to admit that he had been a fool.

The Ugly Duckling

Fairy Tale Classics

retold by Dandi

Proud Mother Duck watched her beautiful babies hatch. One by one, they cracked through their eggshells.

"Peep! Peep!" they cried. "What a large world this is!" So it seemed to them after such a long time in an eggshell.

Only one egg remained – the largest. Mother Duck wondered if it would ever hatch!

At last the egg cracked. Out toddled the largest, ugliest duckling Mother Duck had ever seen! She nudged him into the water with the rest, and loved him just the same.

"Perhaps he's really a turkey," said an elderly duck.

"Looks like a turkey to me!" shouted a drake.

The poor Ugly Duckling, embarassed and ashamed, ducked his head under the water as Mother Duck hurried her flock along.

he next day, a proud Mother Duck showed her fledglings around the barnyard.

"What lovely ducklings!" said the fanciest duck in the yard. "Squawk! Except for that ugly duckling! Get him out of my sight!"

The Ugly Duckling hung his head low. "What should it matter what I look like?" he asked his mother as she wrapped her wings around him in comfort.

fter that, the Duckling's brothers and sisters turned against him.

"Why can't you look like the rest of us?" complained one sister.

"I wish the cat would take you!" quacked his brother.

Even Mother Duck began to feel ashamed that her Ugly Duckling did not look like the others.

"Why can't you accept me as I am?" replied the Ugly Duckling.

*L*ife grew harder for the Ugly Duckling. The others pecked and teased him constantly, until one day, feeling very much alone, he scrambled over the barnyard fence and landed in a flock of songbirds.

"Help!" cried the songbirds. "A monster is after us!"

"I may not look like you," said the Ugly Duckling, "but I am no monster. I'm just different." But his explanation did not stop the songbirds from running away, and the Ugly Duckling was left alone again.

As time passed, leaves changed to yellow, and the grass to brown. One day while wondering through a grassy field, the Duckling came upon a flock of wild geese. He wondered if these new creatures would accept him as he was.

But before the Duckling could try to make friends, shots sounded from hunters' rifles and scattered the flock. The Ugly Duckling hid alone in the tall weeds until it was safe for him to move on.

The Ugly Duckling finally settled on a small secluded pond. As the wind grew colder, the water turned to ice, and he had to keep swimming so he would not freeze. Every night his circle of water grew smaller and smaller. It was a long, cold winter, and the Ugly Duckling felt more alone than ever.

ne night, as the Ugly Duckling waddled through the melting pond, he heard a cry. From the bushes in a nearby field rose a flight of the most beautiful birds he had ever seen. They were dazzling white, with magnificent wings. Their long necks bent gracefully as they flew away. The Duckling could not imagine what creatures they might be. He knew these exquisite beings would only run from him too. Watching them took his breath away.

As Spring arrived the Duckling noticed that the flowers were in bloom, and the grass and leaves turned green again. He had also been growing and changing.

The Ugly Duckling heard the robins singing and felt the warm sunshine on his body. He stretched his wings to feel the radiant day and to his surprise was lifted into the air, floating on a high wind. He gracefully landed in a serene lake beside a beautiful orchard. Nearby swam three beautiful long-necked birds. He recognized them as the elegant creatures he had seen before.

The Ugly Duckling felt sure these beautiful birds would chase him away. But they simply bowed their long necks in a friendly greeting.

'I shall bow too,' he thought. And when he did, he saw with amazement that he looked just like the other birds!

"A new swan!" squealed a little girl on a nearby bank. "More beautiful than the rest!"

The Ugly Duckling had transformed into a magnificent swan. And he proudly joined the flock. But he never allowed the beautiful birds to call those who were different from them ugly.

The Three Little Pigs

retold by Diane Stortz

Fairy Tale Classics

nce there was a mother pig who sent her three little pigs out into the world to seek their fortunes.

"Now remember, boys," she said. "The first thing each of you must do is build a house to keep yourself safe and warm."

own the road went the first little pig. He met a man with some straw and asked the man to give him a bundle. Then he built himself a little house of straw.

own the road went the second little pig. He met a man with some sticks and asked the man to give him a load. Then he built himself a little house of sticks.

The third little pig went on down the road until he met a man with some bricks.

"Bricks make a safe, warm house," said the pig. He asked the man to give him a load. Then he built himself a little house of bricks.

A big, bad wolf had heard the news that three little pigs had gone out into the world to seek their fortunes. The wolf was hungry. "I'd like to seek my fortune, too," said the wolf. "And a pig for supper is a fine place to start."

First, the wolf knocked on the door of the little straw house and said, "Little pig, little pig, let me come in."

"Not by the hair of my chinny chin chin," said the pig.

"Then I'll huff and I'll puff and I'll blow your house in," said the wolf. And he huffed, and he puffed, and he blew down the little straw house. But the first little pig ran to safety inside the house of sticks built by his brother.

Soon the wolf knocked on the door of the little stick house, and said, "Little pig, little pig, let me come in."

"Not by the hair of my chinny chin chin," said the second little pig.

"Then I'll huff and I'll puff and I'll blow your house in," said the wolf. And he huffed, and he puffed, and he blew down the little stick house. This time both little pigs ran to safety inside the house of bricks built by their brother.

oon the wolf knocked at the door of the little brick house and said, "Little pig, little pig, let me come in."

"Not by the hair of my chinny chin chin," said the third little pig.

"Then I'll huff and I'll puff and I'll blow your house in," said the wolf. So he huffed, and he puffed, but he could not blow the house down.

The wolf could see that all this huffing and puffing was not going to get him a pig for supper.

"Little pig," called the wolf. "Do you like turnips?"

"Oh, yes," said the first little pig.

"Then go with me tomorrow to Farmer Smith's turnip field. I will call for you at six o'clock."

"All right," the first little pig said sweetly. But he got up at five, went to the turnip field by himself, and carried home plenty of turnips. He was safely inside his house with his brothers when the wolf came at six o'clock.

he wolf was angry but he tried not to show it. "Little pig," he called. "Do you like apples?"

"Oh, yes," said the second little pig.

"Then come with me tomorrow to the apple orchard on the hill. I will call for you at five o'clock."

"All right," the second little pig said sweetly. But he got up at four o'clock, went to the apple orchard by himself, and carried home plenty of apples. He was busy baking an apple pie when the wolf arrived at five.

he wolf was angry but he tried not to show it.

"Little pig," he called. "Do you like fairs?"

"Oh yes," said the third little pig. "I love to go to fairs."

"Then go to the country fair with me. I shall call for you tomorrow at three o'clock."

"All right," the third little pig said sweetly. But he got up early and went to the fair by himself. He played the games, ate cotton candy, and bought a barrel to hold rainwater.

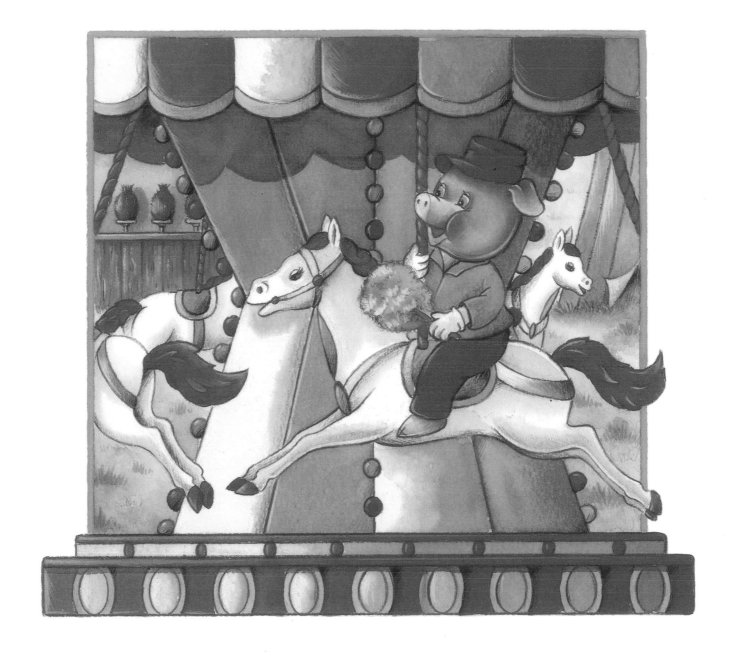

He was rolling the barrel toward home when he saw the wolf coming. When he jumped inside the barrel to hide, it began to roll straight at the wolf. The wolf was terrified by the loud, rolling barrel and he turned and ran straight for home.

The wolf was running out of patience and ideas. He climbed up on the roof of the little brick house.

hen the wolf felt the heat rising up through the chimney, he decided to have cornmeal mush for supper instead of pig. So he went away, and that was the end of the big, bad wolf...but not the end of the story. The three little pigs lived a long and happy life in the little brick house, where they were always safe and warm. (Thanks for the good advice, Mom!)

The Little Mermaid

Fairy Tale Classics

retold by Dandi

In the deepest, bluest sea lived an old Sea King and his six daughters — sea princesses come to be known as mermaids. The youngest princess was by far the most beautiful. When she sang, no sound in the sea or on land could compare with the melody. But the Little Mermaid longed for the world above.

On her fifteenth birthday, the Little Mermaid was granted permission to rise out of the sea and sit on the rocks in the moonlight. She watched as ships passed by. On one ship sailed a handsome, young Prince. When he laughed, the Little Mermaid felt her heart ache with a new longing.

Suddenly a storm wind blew. Lightning cracked. The sails on the Prince's ship billowed. Great waves rose in the sea, pounding against the little ship and tossing it from side to side. The ship began to sink.

The Little Mermaid saw her beautiful Prince thrown into the sea. Diving deep under water, she rescued the Prince and cradled his head in her arms. Then she carried him through the stormy sea to the shore. When she reached the edge of the beach, the storm had calmed. She pushed the Prince onto dry land and kissed the water from his face.

he Little Mermaid heard someone coming. She dove into the sea and hid in the seaweed. A beautiful young woman rushed to the Prince's side. "Well, aren't you handsome!" the girl said softly. "And rich too, if I don't miss my guess. It's about time good fortune came my way."

The Mermaid watched with deep sorrow as the girl and her friends carried the Prince away.

The Little Mermaid returned to the Sea Kingdom, but she could think of nothing but the Prince above. Gathering all her courage, she swam to the domain of the sea witch to find some way to join her love.

"I will give you what you want," cackled the witch. "But the price will be high. If this Prince loves you more than all others, you will remain in his world. If, however, the Prince loves another more than you, then on his wedding day, you shall join the spirits in the heavens. And for this bargain, you must give me the most valuable thing you possess – your beautiful voice!"

he Little Mermaid agreed eagerly. She fell into a deep sleep.
When she awoke, she felt a strange sensation in her fin.
But when she looked, her fin had been transformed into perfect,
human legs!

Before her stood the Prince, his clear, blue eyes fixed on
her. When she opened her mouth, she found she had no voice.
"You poor, lovely creature," he said. Then he carried her to his castle.

hat did you drag in from the sea this time?" said a horrible voice. The Little Mermaid turned to see the very girl she had seen the night the Prince was shipwrecked.

"This is my bride-to-be," the Prince said apologetically to the Little Mermaid. "She saved me when my ship wrecked at sea."

Then the Mermaid had come for nothing! The Prince believed someone else had rescued him. She thought her heart would break.

The next week, the Prince had spent much of his time with the Little Mermaid. They rode horses together and laughed together. Although she tried not to, she fell even more in love with him. The Prince's wedding day grew nearer.

inally the day of the wedding arrived. The bride-to-be had never shown the slightest kindness to the Mermaid, and on her wedding day she was worse than ever. "You are only here because the Prince feels sorry for you," she told the Little Mermaid. "After the marriage is final, I will not allow you in my palace."

The Little Mermaid ran from the palace to the edge of the sea. There she cried until she thought her tears could fill the sea itself.

The Little Mermaid felt someone's hands rest on her shoulders. She knew without looking up that it was the Prince.

"Please don't cry, my sweet. I heard what she said to you. It's okay." He turned her face to his so she could look into his clear, blue eyes. Then he continued, "Today has only made me realize what my heart already knew full well. It is you I love! I knew the first day the sea brought you to me."

he Little Mermaid could hardly believe all that was happening to her. The wedding day went ahead as planned – only she herself became the Prince's bride.

The Prince declared his vows of love, and they were pronounced husband and wife. They kissed; and at the touch of the Prince's lips, the spell of the evil sea witch was broken.

"I love you!" the Little Mermaid cried to her Prince. For the Prince's love had restored her melodious voice. She sang the most beautiful love song imaginable. And she and the Prince lived happily ever after.

Puss in Boots

retold by Diane Stortz

Fairy Tale Classics

nce there was a miller who had three sons. When the miller died, the oldest son became the owner of the mill, the middle son became the owner of the donkey, and the youngest son was left with only the cat.

My brothers can grind wheat with the mill and take grain to market on the donkey," said the youngest son. "But whatever will I do with this cat?" The cat had never been good for anything more than catching mice.

The young man was feeling quite sorry for himself (which was foolish, considering what was about to happen).

T hat's enough complaining," said the cat. "Get me some boots, and I will be able to help you." Surprised to hear the cat speak, the young man hurried off to the shoemaker's and came back with a pair of boots just the right size. The cat put them on and stood up. He was now Puss in Boots.

ow I need a cloth sack with a cord at the top," said Puss in Boots. He filled the sack with grains of wheat and walked out of the house with the sack flung over his back. He went straight to the forest, where he opened the sack and laid it on the ground.

The cat hid behind a tree and waited. Soon, some fat partridges came by and wandered right into the sack. Quickly the cat pulled the sack shut and flung it over his shoulder again.

This time the cat went straight to the king's castle. He bowed low before the king and said, "My master, the Duke of Carabas, sends you his regards and these pretty partridges."

Now the king loved to eat partridges for supper. He had never heard of the Duke of Carabas (of course not--there was no such person). But he thanked Puss in Boots for the lovely present and told him to fill his sack with gold for his master.

he miller's son was amazed when he saw the gold.

Puss in Boots went hunting partridges every day after that. At the king's castle, he became a favorite guest...always allowed to make himself at home. One day, while lying by the hearth in the king's kitchen, he heard that the king and the princess would be taking a carriage ride around the lake that afternoon.

he cat ran home and said to his master, "Quick! You are going swimming!" By this time, the young man was more than happy to do whatever the cat told him. So he hurried to the lake, undressed, and jumped into the water. The cat took his clothes and hid them away.

Just then the king's carriage came into view. The cat stood by the side of the road and began to wail, "Oh, help! Help! My master is freezing. Someone stole his clothes while he was swimming in the lake and he cannot come out of the water."

he king recognized Puss in Boots and ordered the carriage to stop. One of his servants took a blanket to the miller's son, and another servant raced back to the castle for a suit of clothes.

When he was dry and dressed in the splendid clothes, the miller's son certainly looked like a duke. The king believed that he was the Duke of Carabas and invited the young duke to ride in the carriage, which pleased the princess. She was happy because the young man was so handsome.

Puss in Boots was very happy with the way events were working out. He ran ahead of the carriage: first to a wheat field, then to a meadow, and finally to a forest. In each place, he asked the workers there, "Who owns this land?" Each time the answer was the same: "The ogre, of course." "Well," said the cat. "The king is on his way here. When he asks you the same question, you must say that the owner is the Duke of Carabas. Otherwise the ogre will eat you."

All of the workers were afraid of the ogre and astonished by the cat. So when the king's carriage drove by, the king leaned out of the window and asked, "Who owns this land?" The workers answered him exactly as the cat had told them to do. The king and the princess were pleased to know that the young duke was so wealthy.

Puss in Boots ran on until he came to the ogre's castle. He walked right in and bowed to the ogre. "I have heard," said the cat, "that you can turn yourself into any animal at all. I'm sure you can turn yourself into something ordinary, like a dog or a fox, but I don't believe you can turn yourself into something spectacular, like a lion. I have to be convinced. Show me!"

The ogre was happy to do so. He became a lion so ferocious that even Puss in Boots was afraid--but only for a moment.

"A nice trick," said the cat. "But surely you cannot turn yourself into something very small, like a mouse."

"No problem at all," roared the ogre, and in an instant he was running around the room as a mouse. Puss in Boots had not caught any mice for quite a while, but he caught this one and ate him up with one gulp.

ust then, the cat heard the king's carriage approaching. He ran outside to welcome the king and the princess to the castle of his master, the Duke of Carabas.

The king was amazed by the magnificent building, almost more stunning than his own castle. The young man was amazed by what the cat had done for him.

The duke married the princess, and when the king died, the duke became king.

Puss in Boots was his chief advisor, with time off now and then for catching mice.

The Three Bears

Fairy Tale Classics

retold by Dandi

There once lived a quite content family of bear,
And a most spunky gal who had curls in her hair.
Papa Bear was gigantic, and Mama was tall.
But the wee, little Bear barely made noise at all.

In their little old cottage, those three charming bears
Had three couches, three soup bowls, three beds, and three chairs.
Papa Bear's things were giant, and Baby's were small.
Mama Bear liked the middle-sized stuff most of all.

Then one day Mama Bear made the porridge too hot.

"Let's go walking," she said, "while I cool this hot pot."

So the three furry bears lumbered out for a stroll.

Now we turn to a Golden-Haired girl and her role.

Y ou stay out of that woods!" Goldie's mother would say.

But that girl was determined to have her own way!

So she chanced on Bear Cottage, and our heroine

Tried the windows, the keyhole — and then she walked in!

"Oh I know that I shouldn't, but now that I'm here,

No one's home, and I guess I have nothing to fear."

So she tasted the porridge of big Papa Bear.
"It's too hot!" she cried out. "I had better beware."
Then she tried to eat Mama's, but found it too cold,
Till at last she found Baby's. (That girl was so bold!)
Well, the girl took a bite, and she sat down to sup.
"My, my, this one's just right! I shall eat it all up."

ut this chair is too big, and the other too tall."

So she sat in the small chair and had a small fall!

"All this work makes me tired," that Golden girl said.

Then she walked up the stairs and went straight to a bed.

Well, she didn't like Papa or Mama Bear's bed.

So she lay in the wee, little Bear's bed instead.

hen the bears found the mess in the kitchen, they knew.

"Someone ate from my porridge!"

"Someone ate from mine too!"

And when wee, little bear saw his porridge all gone,

How he fussed and he fumed! Oh, that bear carried on!

Come sit, Son. It's all right," said that huge Papa Bear.

Then he thundered, "I think someone sat in my chair!"

Mama Bear thought so too, so they looked all around.

But when Baby Bear sat, he plopped flat on the ground!

In his wee, little voice (though the volume increases),

He screamed, "Look at my chair! Someone broke it to pieces!"

ell, they ran to the bedroom, each bear to his bed.

And when Papa saw his, he just shook that bear head.

"I know someone's been sleeping in my bed!" he swore.

"And in mine," said his wife in a middle-sized roar.

Baby Bear found the girl sound asleep in his bed.

"I think I've solved the mystery," Baby Bear said.

"I know who," said wee Bear. "And I even know how.

She was sleeping in my bed. And here she is now!"

ell, when Golden-Hair heard that, she opened her eyes.

And that golden-haired girl sure was in for surprise.

At the sight of the bears, Goldie turned tail and ran.

And the family of bears never saw her again.

Thumbelina

retold by Diane Stortz

Fairy Tale Classics

nce upon a time, a small swallow settled in a cozy, little nest above a window in a village in the country of Denmark. Through the winter, the swallow told his wife about his adventures in another land. The swallow's wife loved to hear stories and to tell them, especially stories about the small, magical creatures called fairies. Those who love to listen to the swallow's song first heard this story from him a long time ago...

here was a woman who greatly desired to have a child to love and care for, but she had none. She went to see a fairy. "Do you know where I can get a tiny child to love and care for?" she asked.

"Oh, yes," said the fairy. "Take this barleycorn. Place it in a flower pot. Watch what happens."

he woman thanked the fairy and hurried home with the barleycorn. She planted it in a flower pot. In the morning, a large tulip with its petals still closed was growing in the pot. Through the window shone the rays of the sun, and as the sun warmed the tulip, the petals pushed open. In the center sat a tiny little girl. She was smaller than her thumb, and so the woman called her Thumbelina.

The woman placed Thumbelina among some flowers floating in a shallow bowl of water. During the day, Thumbelina sat on a giant tulip leaf and watched the woman as she did her chores. At night, with a polished walnut shell for a cradle, a flower petal for her mattress, and a rose leaf for a blanket, Thumbelina slept quite comfortably.

But one night, an ugly toad got into the woman's house through a broken window. The toad hopped up onto the table and found Thumbelina sleeping in her little boat.

"Whatever she is, she is very beautiful," said the toad. "She would make a lovely wife for my son." With that, the toad carried the sleeping Thumbelina in her walnut shell bed to his home beside the stream. He set Thumbelina down on a large lily leaf a far distance from the shore. Thumbelina was trapped.

In the morning, all the toads came out to greet her. But Thumbelina did not want to live on the lily pad or marry the toad's ugly son. All she could do was cry.

nder the water, lots of little fish saw and heard what was happening. Together they nibbled on the stalk that held Thumbelina's lily leaf until they cut through it and set the leaf free.

Thumbelina floated away. The stream carried Thumbelina past towns and villages. A butterfly settled lightly on the leaf and kept her company.

But suddenly a giant insect swooped down and carried Thumbelina away! "You are so pretty," he told Thumbelina and he set her on a leaf in his tree and gave her flower nectar for her supper.

When other insects came to see the little
creature, they did not think she was pretty.
"She has only two legs and no feelers,"
they said. "How ugly!" they cried. Sorry
that he had ever found Thumbelina, the
insect flew her down from the tree to a daisy,
left her on the daisy and would have nothing
to do with her. Poor Thumbelina spent the
summer and fall living all alone in the woods.
Her one joy was listening to the swallows'
sweet songs.

Then the long, cold winter came. The birds
flew away, the flowers died, and the trees
lost their leaves. Thumbelina wrapped herself
in a maple leaf to try to keep warm, but it
did not help much when the snow began to fall.

Thumbelina wandered out of the woods into a cornfield. All of the corn had been harvested, but under one of the cornstalks Thumbelina found the door to the home of a field mouse. Thumbelina knocked on the door and asked for something to eat. The field mouse was kind and invited Thumbelina to live with her for the winter. "Just keep my house tidy and tell me stories every evening," said the mouse.

One day, the mouse had a visitor--a large, black, blind mole. Thumbelina shuddered when she met the mole, but she was polite and sang to him as the field mouse asked her to. "He is rich," the mouse told her. "He would make a good husband for you." Thumbelina shuddered again.

The mole was pleased with Thumbelina and her songs. He invited her and the mouse to join him at his home for tea. Holding a piece of phosphorescent wood, that glowed like fire, to light the way, the mole led Thumbelina and the mouse through a long, dark, underground tunnel.

In the tunnel, the three came upon a frozen swallow. The mole and the mouse paid the swallow no mind, but Thumbelina was saddened by the sight. That night, she wove a blanket of straw and covered the swallow with it. "Thank you for your songs in the summer," she told the bird gently.

Suddenly the bird opened his eyes! He was not dead, only frozen, and Thumbelina's kindness had revived him.

Then spring came, the swallow was strong enough to fly again. Thumbelina made a hole in the roof of the tunnel so the bird could fly away. "Please come with me," sang the swallow.

The mole wanted to marry Thumbelina and the mouse was determined that he would. Thumbelina spent hours spinning lace for a wedding dress, while the mole made plans for an early winter wedding. Thumbelina was sad.

On the morning of the wedding day, the mole arrived to escort Thumbelina to his underground home. Thumbelina ran outside once more to say goodbye to the sun, which she might never see again.

Just then the swallow flew by. Thumbelina saw him and burst into tears.

"Come with me now," begged the swallow. "I am headed to warmer lands where it is always summer and there are always flowers. You saved my life; now let me save yours!"

This time Thumbelina agreed to go and climbed up onto the swallow's back. Together they made the journey to a beautiful land filled with flowers and fruit. The swallow showed Thumbelina his nest on top of a splendid white castle. Then he set her down among the flowers to find a home. Thumbelina chose a perfect white lily.

To her surprise, a little man was standing in the middle of the lily. He was the flower king. How handsome he is, thought Thumbelina. How lovely she is, thought the flower king. He took his golden crown and set it on Thumbelina's head. Suddenly there were fairies everywhere, clapping their hands. They brought Thumbelina a pair of silvery fairy wings and pinned them on.

Thumbelina married the flower king and became the flower queen. The swallow sang at their wedding. Then, because winter was over in Denmark, he flew back there and told this story to his wife.

And now I have told it to you!

The Gingerbread Boy

Fairy Tale Classics

retold by Dandi

nce a little old woman who had no child –

Cried out to her husband, so meek and mild,

"I would give all I have just to have a son."

So her husband suggested she go bake one.

First she whipped up the batter and beat in eggs.

Then she formed two dough arms and stretched two dough legs.

For the mouth, she made icing and fixed a smile.

Then she added some buttons of cloves for style.

But I have no more raisins to use for his eyes!"

So the man brought her peppercorns just the right size.

"Let me see," said the woman. "The doughboy must bake."

So she turned up the heat for the gingerbread's sake.

hen she opened the oven, she saw to her joy,

"It's a plump and delicious, a Gingerbread Boy!"

But the Gingerbread Boy with a mind of his own,

Yelled, "It's too hot in here! I can make it alone!"

"I can run so fast! Anyone can see.

I'm the Gingerbread Boy, and you can't catch me!"

So after the Boy ran the little old man,

Then the little old woman, a-waving her fan!

But that Ginger Boy ran, though he knew he was wrong,

Through the meadows and fields, as he sang out his song:

"I can run so fast! Anyone can see.

I'm the Gingerbread Boy, and you can't catch me!"

Well, he ran past a cow who was chewing her cud.

And he laughed as he splattered that cow with his mud.

Then the cow gave a chase, and they ran past a pig,

Till the line that was following grew rather big!

 can run so fast! Anyone can see.

I'm the Gingerbread Boy, and you can't catch me!"

Now that Gingerbread Boy found himself at a lake.

"Tell me, what shall I do for my gingerbread's sake!"

As a sly Fox crept by, Sly Fox spied Gingerbread.

"Hop aboard, and I'll swim you!" the old sly Fox said.

On the Fox sat the foolish young Boy Gingerbread.

And as Sly Fox swam on, he cried, "Move up my head!"

So the Gingerbread Boy climbed to Sly Fox's nose.

And that's just what Fox wanted, now don't you suppose?

Sly Fox opened his mouth. Ginger Boy slid right in!

Now our story should end here with Sly Fox's win.

But remember those peppercorns – Ginger Boy's eyes?

When the Fox bit on those, he received a surprise!

Sly Fox sneezed! When he did, the Boy sailed through the air.

And the little old woman stood open-armed there.

They lived happily after, those three, in great joy -

The old woman, the man, and the Gingerbread Boy!

The Jungle Book

retold by Diane Stortz

Fairy Tale Classics

On a warm, summer evening deep in the jungle in India, Mother and Father Wolf and their four cubs awoke from a nap in their cave.

Mother Wolf pricked up her ears. "Listen!" she said. "Something is coming up the hill."

he bushes rustled. Father Wolf was ready to pounce on the intruder. Suddenly, he relaxed. "Look!" he said. "It is a man cub."

Soft and smooth and barely big enough to walk, the little boy looked up at Father Wolf and laughed. Father Wolf picked him up gently and carried him inside.

"How little! How sweet and how brave!" said Mother Wolf softly. The little man cub pushed his way between the wolf cubs to get warm.

W as there ever a wolf mother with a man cub among her children?" asked Mother Wolf.

"I have heard of such things," said Father Wolf. "But never before among the wolves of our pack."

Suddenly the wolves heard a low growl. It was Shere Khan, the tiger, and he was too big to fit through the mouth of the cave. "Give me the man cub. He is mine," said the tiger. But the wolves would not turn over the man cub, and Shere Khan angrily went away. Mother Wolf named the man cub Mowgli.

The law of the jungle said that all wolf cubs old enough to stand must be brought to the pack council, held at the full moon, to be identified. Father Wolf took Mowgli and his own four wolf cubs to the meeting of the pack at Council Rock. Mowgli and the cubs played with pebbles that shone in the moonlight while the other wolves sat around them in a circle.

ith the wolves at this meeting was Baloo, the sleepy old brown bear who ate only nuts and roots and honey. Baloo was the teacher of all the wolf cubs. "Let the man cub run with the pack," said Baloo. "I will teach him the ways of the jungle."

In the distance, behind Council Rock, the growls of Shere Khan could be heard. Then Bagheera, the inky black panther, spoke. "Accept the man cub," Bagheera said. "I will be his guardian." The wolves all listened to both Baloo and Bagheera, and decided that Father and Mother Wolf should keep the man cub to raise as their own son.

The next ten years were wonderful years for Mowgli. He called the wolves and the other jungle animals his brothers. He played games with the wolf cubs during the day and slept soundly next to them at night. He ate coconuts, and bananas, and sweet pawpaws from the trees of the jungle, and drank from the clear jungle streams. Father Wolf, Baloo, and Bagheera taught Mowgli the ways of the jungle, and when he was old enough, he met at Council Rock with the rest of the pack.

One day, Bagheera had a long talk with Mowgli. "You must be ready," Bagheera said. "Someday Shere Khan will come after you. The only way you can be safe, and keep the jungle safe from Shere Khan, is to return to the man village." This news made Mowgli very sad. But because he loved Bagheera and the other jungle animals, he obeyed.

"I will go from the jungle to my own people," Mowgli said. He went to the cave where he had been raised and said good-bye to Father and Mother Wolf, and to his wolf brothers. They promised to visit him at the edge of the farmlands near the man village. And Mowgli promised that someday he would return to the jungle.

hen Mowgli reached the man village, a rich woman named Messua gave him a long drink of milk and some bread. Messua and her husband decided that Mowgli should stay with them. "I might as well," Mowgli said to himself. "At least until I have learned man's language." In the jungle, Mowgli had learned to imitate the sounds of many of the animals, and before dark he had learned the names of many of the things in the house.

oon Mowgli could speak man's language well. He learned to wear clothes, to count money, to farm, and to herd buffalo. But, his wolf brothers still met him at the edge of the farmlands to run and play and tell him the news of the jungle.

One day, Gray Brother brought news that Shere Khan was once more looking for Mowgli, just as Bagheera had warned. "He plans to wait for you at the village gate this evening," said Gray Brother.

ut before the tiger could find Mowgli, Mowgli surprised the tiger. Riding on the back of a buffalo, and with help from Gray Brother, Mowgli herded all the buffalo toward the village gate. The tiger was so surprised and frightened that he ran away without a fight.

owgli took the buffalo back to the man village. Then he said good-bye to the family that had taken him in, and returned to the jungle...his true home. What a happy meeting there was at Council Rock that night! And for the rest of his life, Mowgli lived in the jungle with Baloo and Bagheera and Gray Wolf and the other wolves for company.

The Town Mouse and the Country Mouse

Fairy Tale Classics

retold by Dandi

 y story begins with two homes and two mice.

To tell the whole story, I must tell it twice.

In the thick of the thickets, an old country house

Housed a youngster who went by the name of Pam Mouse.

"It's so boring out here," she complained to the sheep.

"Why, there's nothing to do here but lie down and sleep!"

o she lay in a meadow beside a clear stream,

And she stared at the mountains and started to dream.

"Oh, if only I lived in the city, I know

I would never be bored! I would never feel low."

Far away in a town, in a big boardinghouse,

Lived a cousin of Pam's who was called Hot Rod Mouse.

Hot Rod Mouse told his mom, "I'm so sick of this place!

How I long for the country – the wide open space!"

So he wrote to his cousin and put it this way:

Cousin Pam, Let's trade places for more than a day.

Then he sealed up his letter and licked on a stamp.

And he thought, 'I'll go straight to the country and camp.'

ousin Pam got the letter and hollered out loud!

"I can't wait to see pavement – a real city crowd!"

So she hopped a mouse train that was traveling west.

"Now I'm off to the city, the place I love best!"

n the meantime, the town mouse had boarded his train
To the country, for "City life drives me insane!"
And the first thing he did when he reached the mouse farm,
Was to run from a cow who intended no harm.

I don't care much for chickens. There's no one to play.

And the nearest mouse kid must live twelve miles away.

And the noise that the frogs and the whippoorwills make

Drives me crazy at night as I lie wide awake!"

And the rest of the story? The tale of Pam Mouse?

As to how did she fare in that town boardinghouse?

"Oh the factories and cars and the busses all seethe!

They have houses so close that they can't even breathe!"

How she longed for her meadows and fresh country air!

All the horns and the clatter drove Pam to despair!

And so Hot Rod and Pam traded places once more.

Then they landed back home in the lands they adore.

Now when someone asks, "How did the two homes compare?"

They say, "Nice place to visit. We wouldn't live there!"

Beauty and the Beast

retold by Diane Stortz

Fairy Tale Classics

long time ago, a rich merchant had three daughters. Two were proud, lazy, and thoughtless. But the youngest, named Beauty, was humble, hardworking, and kind.

The merchant lost all his money and had to move his family from a large country estate to a small cottage. The two oldest daughters fretted and complained and caused their father a great deal of grief. But Beauty took care of all of them and never complained. She was a comfort to her father.

ne day, the merchant prepared for a journey to a distant town where he hoped to find work. "Bring us back some fine presents, Father," demanded the two oldest sisters.

"And what would you like, Beauty?" asked the merchant.

Beauty, remembering the lovely gardens at the country estate, said, "I only want your safe return, Father, and a red rose."

On his way to the distant town, the merchant rode into a swirling snowstorm. In the blowing snow he strayed off the path and lost his way. He had almost given up hope of seeing his family again when he smelled roses and felt warm air on his face. He had found an enchanted castle.

There was no one in sight, and no one answered the merchant when he called out, "Hello! Hello! Is anyone here?" The merchant took his horse into the stable, warmed and fed him. Then, tired and hungry, wet and cold, the merchant went inside the castle.

He found a warm, cozy room with a table laid for supper and a fire burning brightly in the fireplace. He ate, feeling all the while that he was being watched, and then he slept.

In the morning, the merchant saw that someone had put out a clean set of clothes for him. He ate and dressed and then went to the stable for his horse. Then he stopped in the gardens and picked a red rose to take home to Beauty.

uddenly, an ugly Beast stood beside him. "Is this how you thank me for my kindness?" roared the Beast. "Have I not given you enough?"

The merchant cowered before the Beast. "Please," he said. "The rose is for my daughter, not for me. I meant no harm."

But the Beast was not moved by the merchant's pleas. "I will spare your life only if you bring your daughter here to live with me," he said.

On despair, the merchant returned home. The next day he brought Beauty to the castle. She was frightened by the Beast's face, but touched by the kindness in his voice.

"Will you live in the castle with me to spare your father's life?" asked the Beast.

"Oh yes, of course," said Beauty.

The Beast gave Beauty's father a chest of gold and told him never to return to the castle. Though it felt as if his heart were breaking, the merchant left Beauty to make the Beast's castle her home.

he Beast gave Beauty her own room, a closet full of lovely gowns, and a clock that woke her by calling her name. Every day Beauty explored the castle, and every night she ate dinner with the Beast. "He is frightful to look at", she thought. "But his manner is gentle and kind". Beauty found that she enjoyed being with the Beast and looked forward to seeing him.

After dinner, Beauty and the Beast strolled through the gardens and continued their quiet conversations. And always, the Beast would look at Beauty and say, "Tell me, Beauty... Am I very ugly?"

es Beast, you are," was always Beauty's reply. "But I am fond of you just the same."

And then the Beast would ask, "Will you marry me, Beauty?"

But though she was fond of him, Beauty could not imagine marrying the Beast.

"No Beast, I can not," was always her reply.

One night in a dream, Beauty saw an ugly old woman. "Do not judge by appearances," the old woman said. "What is ugly on the outside may be beautiful on the inside."

n the morning, Beauty tried to understand her dream, but she could not.

Soon after, the Beast gave Beauty a magic mirror. When she looked into the mirror, Beauty saw her father lying sick in bed. "Oh, Beast!" she cried. "My father needs me! Please let me go home to him."

"Promise to return to me," said the Beast.

"I will," said Beauty.

But she did not. She nursed her father back to health. His business had prospered, and her sisters had grown kinder.

lthough she remembered the Beast fondly and sometimes wished to see him again, she could not bear to leave and break her father's heart again.

Then one night, Beauty looked into the magic mirror the Beast had given her. She gasped. In the mirror she saw the Beast, weak and about to die, under a tree in the castle gardens. Without a word to anyone, Beauty rushed to her horse and rode to the Beast's side.

He was so weak he could not move. Beauty lifted him into her arms and he opened his eyes to look at her one last time.

h Beauty," he said. "Have you come back to me after all?"

"Yes, yes, dear Beast," said Beauty. "Please do not die. I never knew it until now, but I love you."

There was a sudden brilliant light, and then the Beast disappeared and in his place was a handsome prince.

"I was bewitched by a spell that could only be broken by someone who truly loved me in spite of my ugliness," explained the prince.

The prince and Beauty were soon married, and Beauty's father and sisters came to live at the castle, where they all lived happily ever after.

The Princess and the Pea

Fairy Tale Classics

retold by Dandi

There once lived a Prince quite a long time ago,

Who traveled the Kingdom and looked high and low.

"I'm old enough now, and it's quite maddening.

I must find a bride," said the Prince to the King.

"My son," said the Queen. "Now you know that it's true.

There's none good enough in this land – not for you.

You need a *real* princess, for you're such a Prince!"

The Prince knew his mother was hard to convince.

Take that time when the Princess of Mede came to call.

Said the Queen to the Prince, "She's no princess at all!"

Of another fair princess of no small renown –

Said the Queen, "If she's royal, then I'll eat my crown!"

Now the rains came with lightning. That poor palace shook.

So the King and the Queen and the Prince took a look.

At the door, soaking wet from her head to her feet,

Was a Princess who asked in a voice oh so sweet,

"Royal Sirs, Royal Madame, I do not complain.

But wondered if I might come in from this rain."

Well, the Prince, from the moment he saw the fair maid,

Knew that she was the one, though his heart was afraid.

In the meantime, the Princess, quite chilled from the storm,

Cleared her throat. "Is there somewhere that I might get warm?"

Right this way," said the Queen. And the Princess was led
To a room with six mattresses heaped on the bed.
"Do sleep well," said the Queen just as nice as you please.
Then she lifted a mattress and stuck in some peas.

guess that ought to fix her!" then muttered the Queen.

"For if she can't feel that – well, the truth will be seen.

If that Princess can sleep like a little old log,

Then she's no more a Princess than I am a frog!"

ow she tossed and she turned! And though try as she might,

The young Princess, poor girl, got no sleep on that night.

First she said to herself, "There are rocks in this bed.

And I feel so much pain from my feet to my head.

There's no sleep to be had in a bed such as this.

I would bet by my crown jewels that something's amiss."

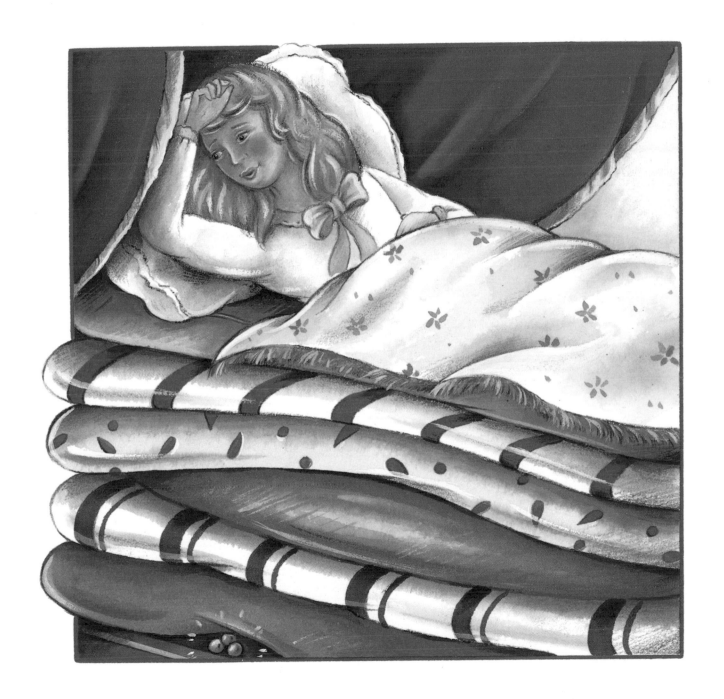

In the morning, she yawned, and she tried to look well.

How she hoped that the King, Queen, and Prince could not tell!

For the girl, too polite to complain of her bed,

Had been raised to be grateful and humble instead.

"You slept well, did you, Princess?" the tricky Queen said.

"I do hope you were comfy. And how was your bed?"

"Oh I don't need much sleep," said the Princess with care.

Then she yawned once or twice and adjusted her hair.

ell that's it!" said the Queen, as she showed her the door.

But the Prince could not take it, not one minute more!

"But, I love her!" he said. "She's the Princess for me!

And so what if the Princess could not feel the pea!"

"Ah, so *that's* what those lumps were!" the Princess said next.

"I neglected to mention. I thought you'd be vexed."

So the Prince and the Princess were married that day.

And they built a fine castle not too far away.

And whenever the King and the Queen came to call,

Why, the Princess surprised her dear mother-in-law.

For the mattress the Queen built (with peas still inside),

The old Queen slept on that, with the King by her side.

And the minute that Queen laid her head on the bed,

She was out like a light, sleeping soundly, they said.

Rumpelstiltskin

retold by Diane Stortz

Fairy Tale Classics

ong ago, there lived a tailor who was known for his bragging...even about things that were not true. This man's talk got his beautiful young daughter into a great deal of trouble. The story would not have a happy ending at all, if not for a faithful servant and a funny little man named... but that's what this story is about.

One day, the tailor happened to see the king riding through town. The man wanted to make himself seem important, so he called to the king, "I have a daughter who can spin straw into gold!" The king stopped at once. "That is an art that pleases me!" he said. The king was a greedy man who was never happy and always wanted more. "Bring your daughter to the castle tomorrow," the king told the tailor. "And I will put her to a test."

The next day, the tailor took his beautiful daughter to the castle. Of course she did not know how to spin straw into gold, but she was shown into a room filled with straw. The king gave her a spinning wheel and a spindle. "Now, to work!" he said. "If all this straw isn't gold by morning, you will never see your father again." Then the king left and locked the door.

The poor girl sat down on the straw and began to cry. Then the door opened again, and a funny little man came into the room.

 ood evening, dear girl," said the little man. "Why are you crying?"

"I am supposed to spin straw into gold for the king," said the girl. "And I don't know how." "Oh, but I know how," said the little man. "What will you give me if I spin it for you?" "My necklace," said the girl.

The little man took the necklace and sat down at the spinning wheel. In seconds, the first spool was full of golden thread. The tailor's daughter fell asleep. When the straw was turned to gold, the little man disappeared.

On the morning at sunrise, the king returned. When he saw the golden spools, he was pleased. But because he was greedy, he took the girl to a larger room filled with more straw. "Spin all this straw into gold by morning if you want to see your father again," said the king. Then he left and locked the door.

Once again the girl began to cry, and once again the door opened and in walked the funny little man.

"What will you give me if I spin the straw into gold for you this time?" he asked.
"The gold ring on my finger," said the girl.
The little man took the ring and began to work.
By morning all the straw was spun into gold.

he king came at sunrise. "Wonderful, my dear!" he cried. But the greedy king wanted still more. He locked the girl in an even bigger room full of straw and told her, "Spin all this straw into gold tonight. If you do, you shall become my wife."

hen the king was gone, the little man came again. "What will you give me this time if I spin the straw into gold for you?"

"I have nothing left to give you," the girl said sadly. "Then promise to give me your first child after you become queen," said the little man. The tailor's daughter did not believe the king would really marry her. So she promised the little man her first child. In the morning, the king found the room full of gold, and he married the tailor's daughter.

The next year, the queen gave birth to a beautiful child. She was happy, and had forgotten the funny little man. But suddenly he appeared and said, "Now give me what you promised."

The queen was horrified. She offered the little man all the treasure of the kingdom instead. "No," said the little man. "Something living is more important than all the treasure in the world."

Then the queen began to grieve and weep and could not be consoled. The little man began to feel sorry for her. "I will give you three days," he said. "If you can guess my name by the third day, you may keep your child."

The queen spent the night making a list of every name she had ever known. Then she sent a servant out into the kingdom to make a list of names she had never heard before.

When the little man appeared again that evening, the queen began to call out the names one at a time. "Are you Tom? Dick? Harry?" she asked. But after every name the little man shook his head.

"Are you Gaspar? Melchior? Balthasar?" The little man just smiled and said, "That's not my name." The next day the queen sent her servant out into the kingdom to search for unusual names, like Ribsofbeef or Muttonchops or Lacedleg. But when the little man appeared that evening, he just shook his head and said again and again, "That's not my name."

On the third day, the queen was in despair. She sent her servant out into the kingdom one last time. When he came back, the servant said, "I climbed a high mountain, where the fox and the hare say good night to each other at the edge of the forest. There I saw a small cottage, and in front of the cottage was a fire. And in front of the fire danced a funny little man. He hopped about on one leg, singing,

"Today I'll brew, tomorrow I'll bake.
Soon I'll have the queen's namesake.
Oh, how hard it is to play my game,
For Rumpelstiltskin is my name!"

When the queen heard this, she began to dance herself, for joy. When the little man appeared that evening she asked him, "Is your name Kunz?" "No!" said the little man. "Is your name Heinz?" "No!" said the little man. He began to reach for the queen's sleeping child. "Is your name Rumpelstiltskin?" asked the queen.

"Who told you? Who told you?" howled the little man. He jumped around screeching and stomping his feet so hard that he stomped right through the floor and disappeared. And that was the last time anyone ever saw Rumpelstiltskin.

Hansel and Gretel

Fairy Tale Classics

retold by Dandi

retel and her brother Hansel lived near a great forest. One night Gretel awoke to voices. "There is not enough food," screamed the stepmother. "We must take the children to the woods and leave them."

"Never!" cried their father.

"Would you rather watch your children starve?" persisted the stepmother. She gave her husband no rest, but he would never let harm come to his children.

retel ran and told Hansel of their stepmother's plot. She knew she could count on her big brother.

That night, Hansel sneaked outside. When he came back, his pockets were filled with flint rocks. Gretel held them up to the moonlight and saw them glisten.

"These will guide us home," Hansel said.

arly one morning, the woman snuck the children out of the house. "Get up, you lazy things!" screeched their stepmother. "You must help me gather wood in the forest." Then she led them through the deep woods.

Gretel peeked at Hansel as he dropped flint rocks along their path. When they reached the dense woods, their stepmother disappeared.

"It's all right, Gretel," said Hansel, giving her hand a squeeze. "The rocks will show us the way home."

hen the moon rose, the flint rocks glistened. Hansel and Gretel followed the rocks all the way home.

The next day, their stepmother took them deeper into the woods. Hansel had no time to collect rocks, so he dropped pieces of bread. But when they tried to follow their trail home, they discovered that the birds had eaten the bread!

rightened and confused, Hansel and Gretel wandered in circles until they happened upon a little gingerbread house.

"Hansel, look! A whole house made of gingerbread! And the windows are sugar!" Gretel yelled as she licked the sweet panes.

Hansel broke off a piece of frosting shingle from the roof. Then they heard a voice from inside:

"Nibble, nibble, gnaw all year!
Who is nibbling at my cottage dear?"

he door opened and out came a wrinkled, old woman. Gretel was terrified!

"Come and stay with me, precious ones," said the woman. "I have plenty to eat, as you can see."

That night Hansel and Gretel ate a fine meal and slept on pretty, little beds.

The next day Hansel woke up in a cage! The old woman forced Gretel to cook for her brother. "I'll fatten him up before I eat him!" said the woman.

Gretel wept as she did all that the woman commanded. But when the woman wasn't looking, Gretel handed her brother a chicken bone through the bars of the cage. "The woman is nearly blind," Gretel whispered. "Stick this bone out when the old woman comes to check on you. She'll think it's your finger."

ach day the old woman visited Hansel's cage. "Stretch out your finger that I may feel if you will soon be fat," she ordered. Hansel, however, held out the chicken bone instead. The old woman grew frustrated. Finally she told Gretel, "Fetch me water, for tomorrow I will eat Hansel, fat or lean!"

The next day, Gretel was forced to make a fire in the oven. "Now," said the old woman. "Crawl in to see if it is hot enough."

Gretel knew the woman meant to push her in. So she said, "I don't know how to get in."

"Silly goose!" cried the woman. "Like this!" When the woman crawled into the stove, Gretel slammed the door shut!

Gretel unlocked her brother, and they raced for the door. Hansel tripped over an old chest, spilling out diamonds and rubies. The children stuffed their pockets with the old woman's jewels and ran out of the house.

They followed a nightingale through the woods. When they were almost home, their father came running to them. He threw his arms around them. "My children!" he cried. "When I found out what your stepmother had done, I sent her away. I have been looking for you ever since!"

Gretel and Hansel lived in comfort and joy with their father. And every now and then, Gretel ventured back to the gingerbread cottage – for dessert.

Little Red Riding Hood

retold by Diane Stortz

Fairy Tale Classics

On a small village at the edge of a great forest lived a little girl and her mother. The girl had a red, velvet riding cloak with a hood that her grandmother had made for her. She looked so pretty in the cloak and wore it so often, that the villagers all called her Little Red Riding Hood.

One day, Little Red Riding Hood's mother said, "Take this basket of bread and butter to your grandmother's house for me. Your grandmother has not been feeling well and has not been able to cook for herself."

331

ow the grandmother's house was on the other side of the great forest. Little Red Riding Hood knew the way through the forest, for she went there often. She wasn't the least little bit afraid. But her mother knew that any forest could be dangerous. "Go quickly," she said. "Don't dawdle. And stay on the path."

"I will," said Little Red Riding Hood. And off she went, carrying the basket of bread and butter.

he had not gone far when she saw a wolf.

"Good morning, Mr. Wolf," said Little Red Riding Hood.

"Where are you going?" the wolf wanted to know. "And what do you have in that basket?"

"I am going to my grandmother's house," said Little Red Riding Hood. "I am taking her this bread and butter from my mother, because she has been sick."

ow the wolf hadn't eaten in several days. Bread and butter would make a tasty snack, thought the wolf, but what I really want to eat is a tasty little girl! And I have a plan.

"Since your grandmother has been sick and unable to get out, perhaps she would enjoy a bouquet of wildflowers as well as the food in your basket," suggested the wolf.

ittle Red Riding Hood looked around. The forest was filled with wildflowers of all colors. "Why, that's a lovely idea, Mr. Wolf," said Little Red Riding Hood. "But my mother did tell me not to stray off the path..."

"Well," said the wolf, "I'm certain that if your mother had thought about a bouquet of wildflowers, she would have agreed to let you pick some. Why don't you start with those red ones over there?"

"All right," said Little Red Riding Hood, and she left the path through the forest to wander under the trees looking for flowers.

When the wolf raced down the path to the house where Little Red Riding Hood's grandmother lived, he caught his breath and knocked on the door.

"Who's there?" called the grandmother.

"It's Little Red Riding Hood," said the wolf in a high, squeaky voice. "I've brought you some bread and butter."

"Then lift the latch and come in, dear," said the grandmother. She was tucked into bed and did not want to get up. But when the door opened and the wolf walked in, she sat straight up and then fainted from fright.

The wolf was not interested in eating the old woman, only Little Red Riding Hood. So he rolled the grandmother under the bed. He put on her lacy nightcap and jumped into her bed, pulling the covers up to his chin. Then he waited for Little Red Riding Hood to arrive.

hen Little Red Riding Hood
could not carry any more
wildflowers, she found the path and went
on her way to her grandmother's house.
She knocked at the door.

"Who is it?" called the wolf in his best
grandmother voice.

"It's Little Red Riding Hood," answered
the girl. "I've brought you some bread and
butter and a bouquet of wildflowers."

"Lift the latch and come right in, dear,"
said the wolf.

ittle Red Riding Hood went inside. "Come closer, my dear," said the wolf. Little Red Riding Hood went closer, but not too close.

"My goodness, Grandmother," she said. "What big eyes you have!"

"The better to see you with, my dear," said the wolf.

"And what big teeth you have, Grandmother," said Little Red Riding Hood.

he better to eat you with!" cried the wolf. He sprang out of bed and tried to grab the little girl, but she was too quick for him. She dropped her basket and ran out the door.

A hunter who was passing through the forest saw Little Red Riding Hood run outside with the wolf close behind her. The hunter chased the wolf deep into the forest. When the hunter came back, he went inside with Little Red Riding Hood to help her look for her grandmother. They found her standing beside her bed, looking quite shaken.

he danger is over now," said the hunter.

"The hunter chased the wolf away!" cried Little Red Riding Hood.

"Thank you for saving Little Red Riding Hood, sir," Grandmother said to the hunter. "Please stay and join us for tea."

So the hunter sat down with Little Red Riding Hood, and her grandmother and drank tea and ate bread and butter. And although the bouquet of wildflowers made a lovely centerpiece, Little Red Riding Hood never strayed off the path in the forest again.